# Ballet Star

Written by Nicola Baxter • Illustrated by Gill Cooper

ARMADILLO

One day, little Star's granny took her to a ballet.

It was magical.

Girls in beautiful dresses floated across the stage.
A handsome prince leapt into the air so high
that Star said, "Wow!" and Granny said, "Shhh!"

"That's what I'm going to do when I grow up," said Star.
Her eyes were shining.

Star's mother explained that ballet dancers have to start training when they are very young. "Then I need to start now!" cried Star.

She was already twirling around the sitting room (and knocking over quite a few things).

A week later, Star went to her first ballet lesson.

She wore ...

a pink leotard

a little white skirt

pale pink tights

and pink ballet shoes

Mother pinned her hair back. Star didn't like that much but she did look just like a real ballerina.

"Ballet is hard work," said the teacher. Star frowned.
Those floating girls had made it look easy.

Each week, Star went to her lesson.

She began by standing in first position ...

pointing her toes ...

walking with her head up and her back straight ...

curtseying ...

and balancing ...
over and over again.
It really was
hard work.

Star watched herself in the big mirror. She could see that it was
going to be a long time before she could dance really well.

Star told Granny that she was not very good at dancing.

"I'm sure that's not true," said Granny. "Dancing is a lovely thing for any boy or girl to learn, but it takes years and years. You don't need to wait as long as that to feel like a famous ballerina though. All you have to do is imagine."

Now, when Star goes to sleep, she imagines people cheering as she twirls and floats across the stage. "Wow!" cry all the people (and no one says, "Shhh!")

And Star smiles. She always knew she was a true ballet star. Are you a star, too?